W9-APG-951

DISNEY·PIXAR

Adapted by Jenny Miglis

Ding-dong! It was Andy's birthday, and the guests had begun to arrive. Andy ran downstairs to open the door. As soon as he left his room, his toys came to life!

Andy's favorite toy, Woody the talking cowboy, called a meeting. "Every Christmas and birthday we go through this," he explained to the nervous toys. "No one is getting replaced."

Still, the toys waited anxiously until Andy burst into the room with his brandnew toy—Buzz Lightyear, space ranger. Carefully, he placed Buzz on his bed against the pillow. Woody gulped—that was *his* spot! Then Andy ran back downstairs to the party.

The toys were all thrilled with Buzz's cool buttons and flashy lasers.

"That's enough!" Woody cried. He was upset with all the attention the space ranger was getting. "Look, we're all impressed with Andy's new toy."

"Toy?" Buzz questioned. "I think the word you're searching for is space ranger." He thought he was the *real* Buzz Lightyear, not a toy. To prove himself, he cried, "To infinity and beyond!" and leaped off the bed.

Buzz bounced off a ball onto a race car, which zoomed him up to a mobile. He grabbed it, soared around, and landed back on the bed. It looked like he really *could* fly!

"That wasn't flying," Woody scoffed. "That was falling with style."

The next evening, Andy was allowed to bring *one* toy with him to Pizza Planet. Woody *really* wanted to be that toy. He had a plan to get Buzz out of the way.

"Down there—a helpless toy," Woody called to Buzz. "It's trapped!"

As Buzz looked for the toy, Woody rammed RC Car into the spaceman. But instead of falling between the desk and the wall as the cowboy had hoped, Buzz fell out the window! The other toys watched in horror as Buzz plummeted to the ground.

"This was no accident," Mr. Potato Head said, turning toward Woody. "You couldn't accept that Buzz might be Andy's new favorite toy so you got rid of him!" The toys were very upset with Woody.

Just then, Andy came in, looking for his new toy. When he couldn't find Buzz, he grabbed Woody and headed to the car.

Outside, Buzz scrambled onto the car's bumper just as it drove away. When the car stopped, Buzz climbed inside.

"Buzz! You're alive!" Woody exclaimed.

Buzz was mad at Woody. They started fighting and fell out of the car. Then the car pulled away! Luckily, they caught a ride to Pizza Planet in a delivery truck.

There, Buzz climbed inside a spaceship. But the spaceship was really a claw game filled with alien toys. Woody tried to pull Buzz out, but Andy's dreaded neighbor Sid, who tortured toys for fun, was already plucking out Buzz—and Woody!

Later, trapped in Sid's room, Woody and Buzz encountered a group of Sid's mutant toys—a doll's head on a spiderlike body, a car with feet instead of wheels, and many other freaky creations. Buzz and Woody jumped into Sid's backpack to hide.

The next day, Buzz and Woody tried to escape, but Sid's dog, Scud, chased them. Woody ran one way, and Buzz ran another.

As Buzz raced past a TV, he saw a commercial for Buzz Lightyear action figures. At last, he realized the awful truth—he *was* a toy! Buzz made a final attempt to fly but landed in a heap. "I'm a sham!" he cried.

Soon after, Sid strapped Buzz to a small rocket. Then he went to bed, eager to launch Buzz to infinity and beyond the next day.

"Come on, Buzz!" Woody exclaimed from under the crate where he had hidden from Sid. "You can get me out of here, and then I'll get that rocket off you. And we'll make a break for Andy's house!"

Andy's family was getting ready to move to a new house. If Buzz and Woody didn't get home soon, they would be left behind.

"I can't," Buzz replied. "I'm just a toy."

"Next door is a kid who thinks you're the greatest, and not because you're a space ranger. Because you're a *toy*," Woody said.

That convinced Buzz. "Come on, Sheriff!" he cried.

But suddenly, Sid woke up. "Time for liftoff!" he yelled. He grabbed Buzz and raced outside.

Thinking quickly, Woody pleaded with Sid's mutant toys. "There's a good toy down there, and he's going to be blown to bits in a few minutes all because of me. We gotta save him!"

The toys were tired of Sid's gruesome games, so they agreed to help.

Outside, Sid began the countdown: "Ten . . . nine . . . eight . . ." Just as he was about to touch the match to the rocket's fuse, he heard a strange voice. "This town ain't big enough for the two of us."

Sid stared at Woody in disbelief. A cowboy toy was talking to him! Huh? How could a toy talk if no one had pulled its string?

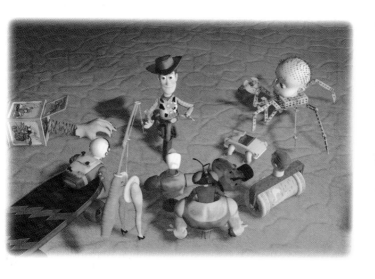

Suddenly, Woody and an army of mutant toys surrounded Sid. They were mad—and they were headed right for him! In a flash, Sid ran screaming into his house, never to mistreat a toy again.

Woody breathed a sigh of relief and looked over at Andy's house. Oh, no! The moving van was pulling away! Woody and Buzz chased after it.

Just as they caught up to the van, Scud attacked! Woody made it safely onto the bumper, but Buzz was left behind. Thinking quickly, Woody sent RC Car to save the space ranger.

"He's at it again!" Rex cried. The other toys still thought Woody had something against Buzz. Now they figured he was trying to get rid of RC Car! Disgusted, they pushed the cowboy off the van.

RC Car picked up Woody and Buzz and raced back toward the van. But then his batteries died! What would they do?

Luckily, Buzz had an idea. "The rocket!" he exclaimed. It was still attached to his back. Buzz and Woody fired it up and—WHOOSH!—it launched into the sky, carrying the toys with it.

"Hey, Buzz, you're flying!" Woody cried.

Buzz laughed. "I'm just falling with style."

The toys landed in the car—safe at last!

After that, all was well in Andy's new home until Christmas, which meant—new toys!

"You're not worried, are you?" Woody teased Buzz. "What could Andy possibly get that is worse than you?"

Arf! Arf! Arf! "A puppy!" Andy cried. The toys looked at each other. Uh-oh!

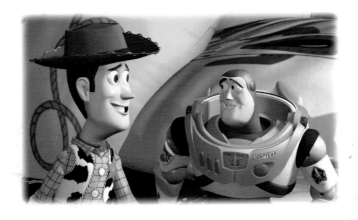